Bartali
Bartali

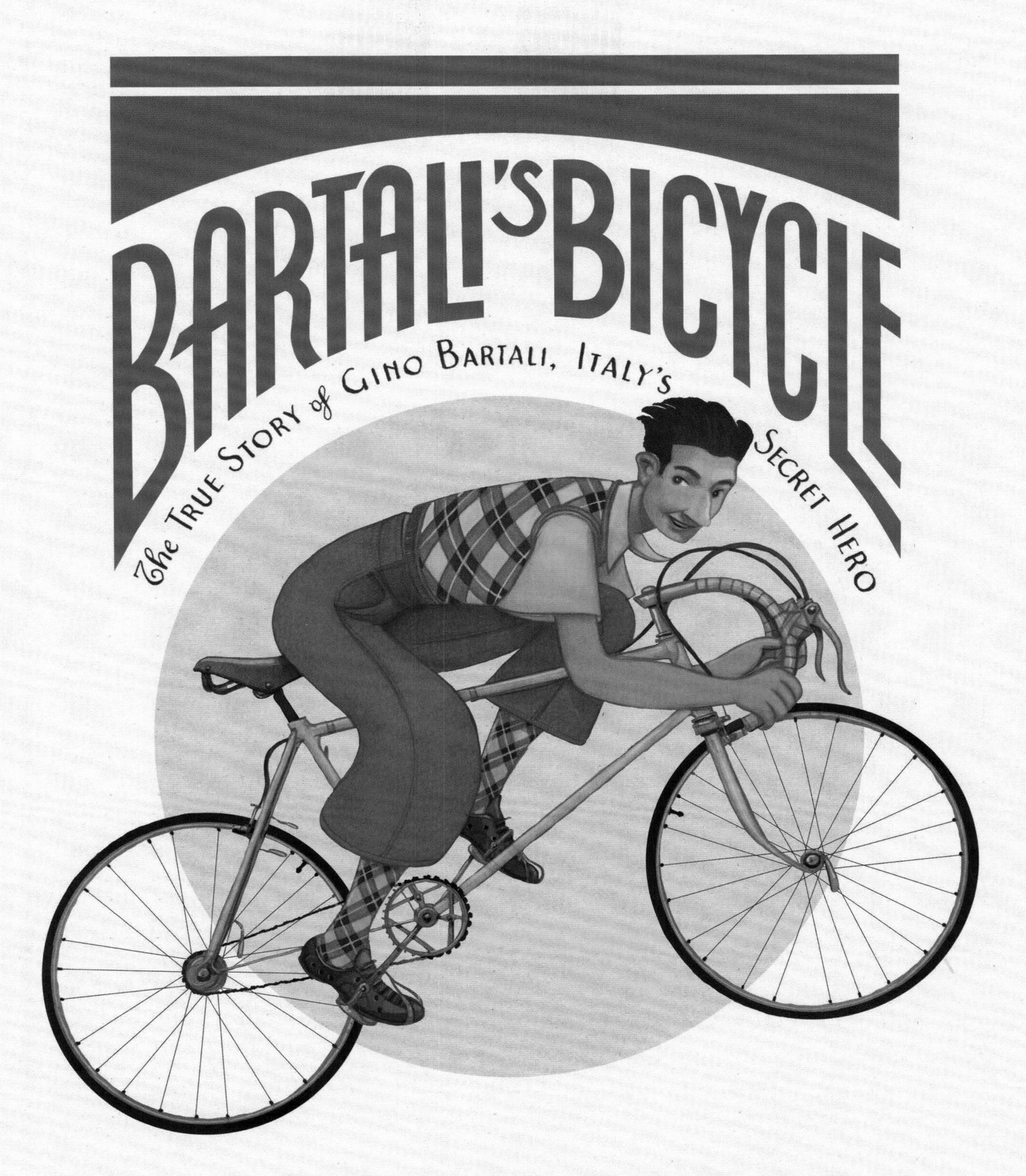


WRITTEN BY MEGAN HOYT
ILLUSTRATED BY IACOPO BRUNO

Quill Tree Books
An Imprint of HarperCollinsPublishers

Gino Bartali hopped onto his bicycle and bounced along the cobblestone streets of Florence, Italy. For years, he had pedaled across these crowded piazzas and narrow avenues—but this day was special.

Today, Gino was to begin training for his first bicycle race.

**Elbows in. Head down.**

**Face to the wind.**

Gino pedaled up steep mountains dotted with alpine villages. He traveled down the coast, where the sea lapped the land and the sun bronzed his skin.

For eight long years, Gino cycled across Italy, memorizing mountain trails and rugged paths. He won race after race. Soon he earned a shelf full of trophies and a jacket full of first-place ribbons.

Then, on a hot July day in 1938, Gino won the biggest race in the world—the Tour de France.

His face was on magazine covers. Cheering crowds mobbed him. Gino Bartali was an international hero!

But Gino said, **"No, no, no! Heroes are those who have suffered. I am just a cyclist."**

# TOUR de FRANCE

After Gino won the Tour de France,

**the world started to change.**

Strange new ideas began to spread across Italy.

Armies marched. Generals barked orders.

Soon all of Europe was at war.

Tanks belched out thick smoke onto Italy's beautiful cobbled streets

**Sirens screeched.**
**Bombs fell.**

And the strange new ideas became even stranger.

A powerful leader said, "People will fall for a big lie more easily than a small one." Then he told a giant lie to the whole world. He said Jewish people were not really human. They must be rounded up and arrested.

Gino was shocked at this news. Many of his closest friends were Jewish. They were scientists, builders, artists, and shopkeepers. They were all good people—every one of them. And Gino's friend Giacomo Goldenberg was like a brother to him.

**Gino refused to believe the lie.**

**Soldiers swarmed into Florence.** It seemed the war would never end, but Gino tried to keep training.

He pedaled past historic cities with leaning towers and giant domed cathedrals. He pedaled past country villages with quaint cottages and rows of grapevines.

Everywhere he went, he saw families who were no longer allowed to live in their homes, work in their shops, or perform in concerts. He saw soldiers push children onto giant trucks while their parents clutched their bellies and cried.

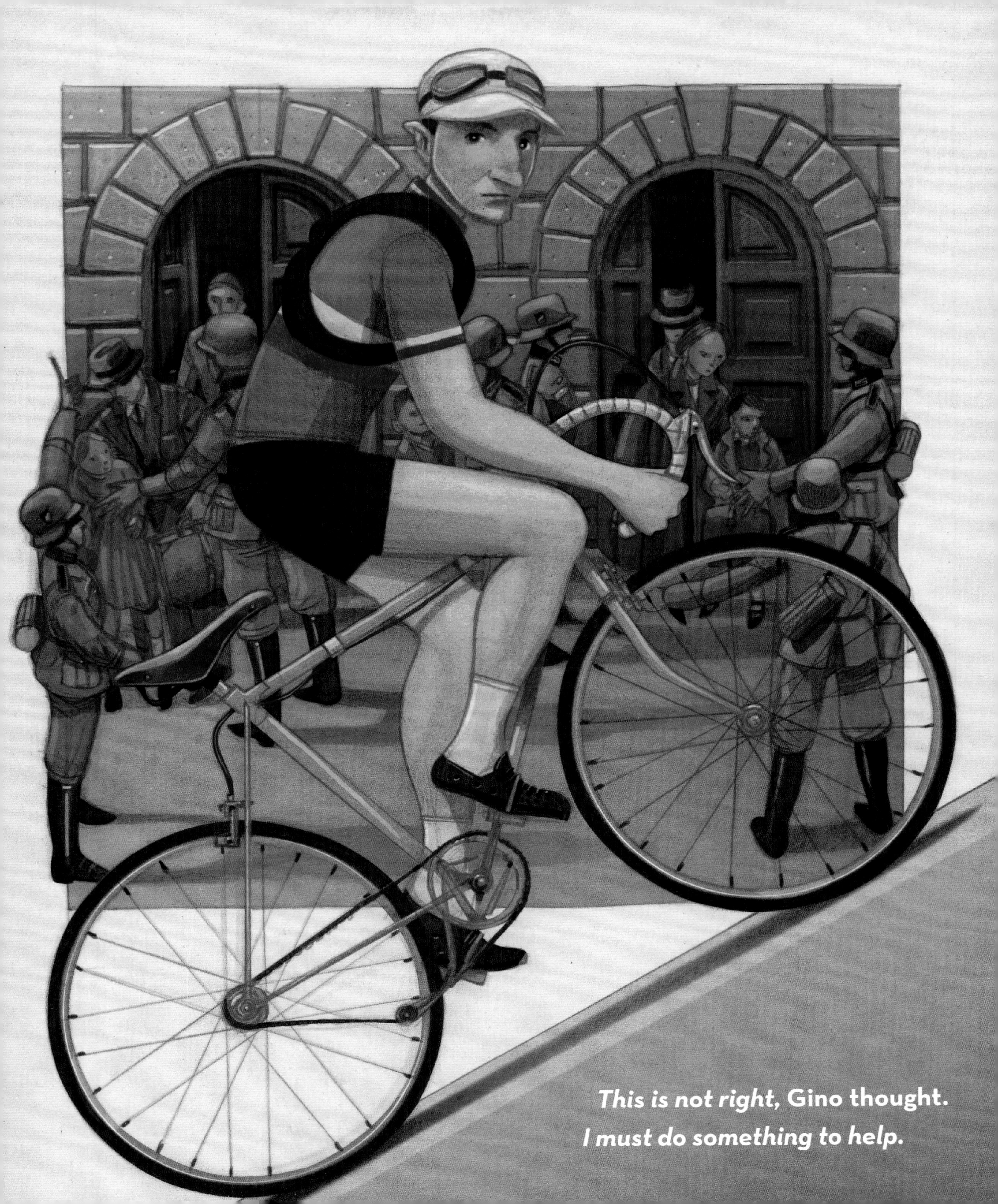

*This is not right*, Gino thought.
*I must do something to help.*

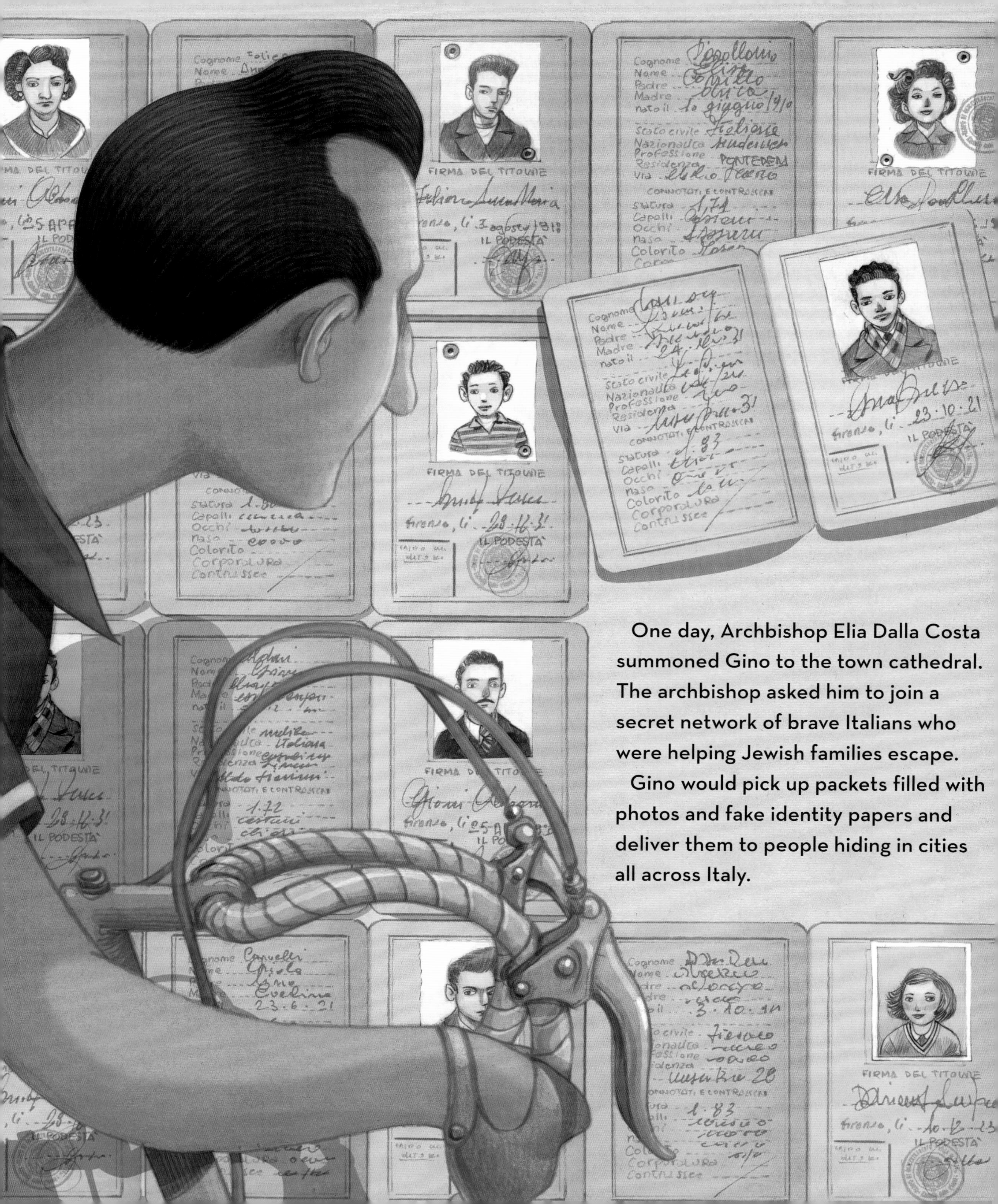


One day, Archbishop Elia Dalla Costa summoned Gino to the town cathedral. The archbishop asked him to join a secret network of brave Italians who were helping Jewish families escape.

Gino would pick up packets filled with photos and fake identity papers and deliver them to people hiding in cities all across Italy.

With new identities, parents could take their children across the mountains into Switzerland or flee to America.

**Gino was afraid.** But he knew this was important—more important than any race he'd ever been in.

He decided to help. "Some medals are pinned to your soul, not your jacket," he said.

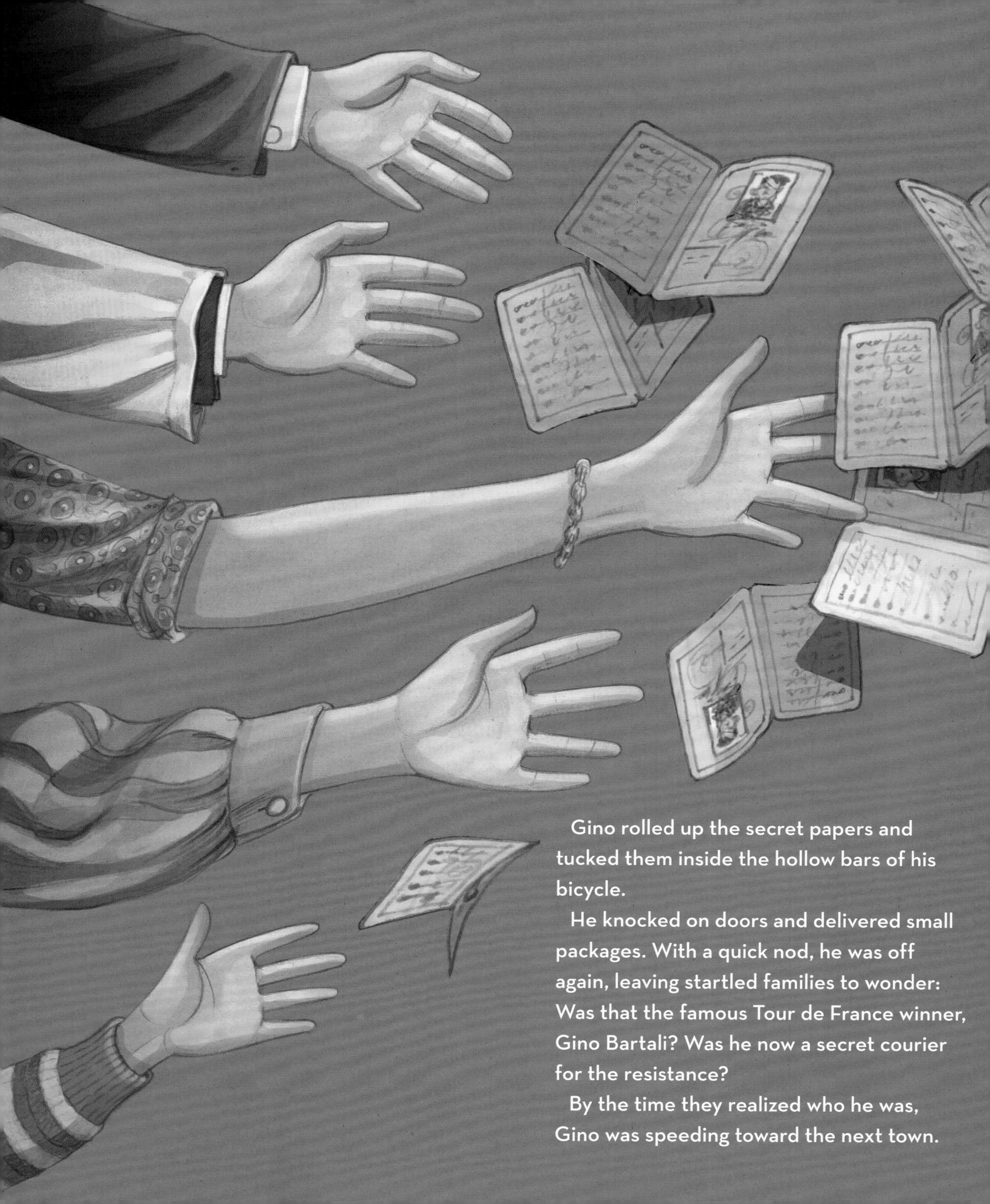

Gino rolled up the secret papers and tucked them inside the hollow bars of his bicycle.

He knocked on doors and delivered small packages. With a quick nod, he was off again, leaving startled families to wonder: Was that the famous Tour de France winner, Gino Bartali? Was he now a secret courier for the resistance?

By the time they realized who he was, Gino was speeding toward the next town.

Elbows in. Head down. Face to the wind. Gino was the fastest cyclist in the world. He could cover 250 miles in a single day! But sometimes it wasn't fast enough. People were packed onto trains and sent away before he could reach them.

**Gino wanted to do more.**

TERONTOLA
Bartali
URSUS

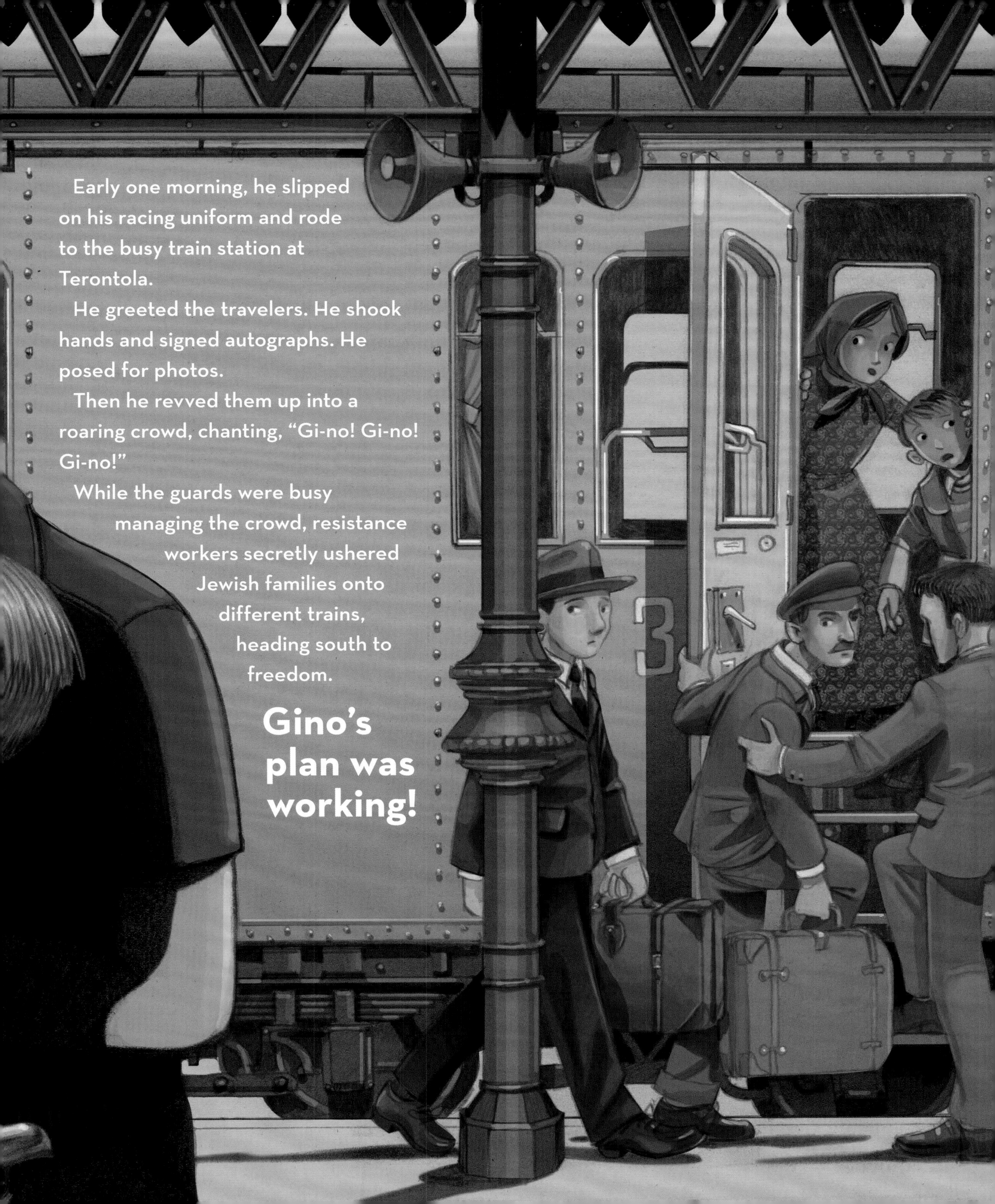

Early one morning, he slipped on his racing uniform and rode to the busy train station at Terontola.

He greeted the travelers. He shook hands and signed autographs. He posed for photos.

Then he revved them up into a roaring crowd, chanting, "Gi-no! Gi-no! Gi-no!"

While the guards were busy managing the crowd, resistance workers secretly ushered Jewish families onto different trains, heading south to freedom.

**Gino's plan was working!**

But there was no time to celebrate. Through the secret resistance network, Gino discovered that soldiers were searching for his friend Giacomo, and every available hiding place was occupied.

**Except one.**

Gino hid the Goldenberg family in his cellar. They would have to sleep four to a bed. They could never step outside or feel the warmth of the sun on their faces. But they would be safe.

Like all strong young men, Gino was forced into the Italian militia. A soldier fighting for the enemy! How could he do such a thing?

Gino met with the leaders of the resistance.

"We have to be cunning," he said. "These are terrible times."

The resistance leader said, "Gino, put on the uniform and go find where they are hiding their prisoners."

Gino knew just where to look. He pedaled back to the rolling hills where he grew up and strolled into the Villa La Selva. Wearing his militia uniform, he left with forty-nine English soldiers.

**And no one noticed!**

With each successful mission, he grew even more daring—

Until one day his secret work almost came to a halt.

Gino was pedaling across an Italian piazza when gunshots rang out. Bombs blasted. People ran for shelter, and Gino was thrown from his bicycle.

His bicycle!

There it was, his secret vault crammed full of lifesaving documents, bent and broken. Papers jutting out from the frame. The identity papers!

**Gino had to act fast.**

He brushed himself off, picked up his bicycle, and ran.

When Gino reached Florence, his beloved city was a battle zone. Enemy troops had destroyed every bridge except one. Gino wondered if the war would ever end. But there was something he did not know.

13
Bartali
Bartali
URSUS

By 1944, people all over the world—ordinary folks of all religions, rich and poor, young and old—joined in the fight against these soldiers whose hearts were filled with hate. They, too, were rescuing Jewish families. And soon, the liar was defeated! The war was over!

Neighbors sprang from their homes and celebrated in the streets.

The Goldenberg family stepped out of the cellar, lifting their faces to the noonday sun. Their hearts soared above the clouds.

**They were free!**

Even though Gino saved the lives of more than eight hundred Jewish people during the war, he kept his story quiet for as long as he lived.

"Good is something you do, not something you talk about," he said.

But stories trickled out. Children came forward.

Grateful families remembered the remarkable Gino Bartali, Tour de France winner, Italian sports hero, international celebrity . . .

And secret champion.

# TIMELINE

| | |
|---|---|
| **JULY 18, 1914** | Gino Bartali is born. |
| **1927** | Gino begins working at a bicycle shop and enters his first race. |
| **1935** | Gino enters his first professional race. |
| **1937** | Gino enters the Tour de France but does not win. |
| **1938** | Gino Bartali wins the Tour de France. |
| **NOV 14, 1940** | Gino marries Adriana Bani in Florence; Cardinal Elia Dalla Costa performs the ceremony. |
| **SEPT 8, 1943** | Nazis occupy Italy. |
| **SEPT 1943** | Gino is summoned to the Duomo (Basilica di Santa Maria del Fiore) by his friend Archbishop Dalla Costa. |
| **OCT 16, 1943** | Nazis begin rounding up all the Jews in Rome. |

*For a year, Gino Bartali cycles across Italy, up to 250 miles each day, rain or shine.*

| | |
|---|---|
| **AUG 1944** | Bartali is arrested, questioned, and released. |
| **OCT 1944** | Italy is freed by the Allies. |
| **1948** | In a surprise victory, Gino Bartali wins the Tour de France a second time. |

*Gino Bartali remains silent about his wartime activities,*
*refusing to talk about anything but cycling at public events.*

| | |
|---|---|
| **MAY 5, 2000** | Gino Bartali dies at age eighty-five in Florence. |

Dear Reader,

My grandfather, Gino Bartali, saved many people during World War II. Through his bravery and smarts, he helped eight hundred Jewish people and about fifty English soldiers, in addition to others who were politically persecuted. The fury against the Jewish community by the Nazi fascists has been a plague for all of humanity. For me, so much cruelty is inconceivable.

Gino would have saved anyone in danger, without considering their country of origin, social level, religion, or politics. He was a man of true courage and deep compassion. Destiny took away the best years of his cycling career during World War II, but as often happens, at the worst moment, he gave his best—his kindness, his life.

Many people have asked me why my grandfather never spoke about his humanitarian work. I believe he spoke by being silent. The good-hearted men and women who offer their lives to save thousands, or even only one, don't need celebrations. A person whose soul is noble doesn't need to emphasize his or her acts. Greatness is shown by working in secret.

I hope my grandfather's story inspires others to be courageous in the face of injustice and to live their lives with the same compassion and quiet strength that he did. Then I will know that his brave heart lives on in the souls of generations to come.

Sincerely,
Lisa Bartali
Granddaughter of Gino Bartali

# AUTHOR'S NOTE

I stepped off the bus in Ponte a Ema, the Florence suburb where Gino Bartali grew up, and there it was, looming high above the curving street—the Gino Bartali Museum of Cycling! Right beside the front desk was a bicycle with a large wagon attached to it. Upstairs, I found more memorabilia. Gino's yellow racing bicycle. His yellow jersey. Newspaper articles about the Tour de France. And a copy of a certificate from Yad Vashem, the Holocaust Remembrance Center in Israel, which declared Gino Bartali "Righteous Among the Nations." Archbishop Elia Dalla Costa also earned this award for hiding more than two hundred people inside his own residence, right in the middle of the bustling city of Florence. Some of them were probably there when Gino met with the archbishop—hiding quietly in closets and storerooms!

Gino was happy to help Archbishop Dalla Costa and the resistance. "This is a war without reason, without honor," he said. But he did not do this dangerous work alone. Gino was part of a secret network called DELASEM (Delegation for the Assistance of Jewish Emigrants). The leaders of the Florence network were Archbishop Dalla Costa; Giorgio Nissim, a Jewish man and an antifascist; and Rabbi Nathan Cassuto. They worked together to save Jewish citizens from the Nazi troops who were pounding on doors and arresting people. From 1939 to 1944, the DELASEM network and the Assisi underground helped more than nine thousand people escape. Because of their courage and commitment, 80 percent of all the Jewish citizens living in Italy before World War II were saved.

Trento Brizi was one of the counterfeiters who created the forged ID cards that helped people escape. When he was interviewed years later, he said, "The idea of taking part in an organization that could boast of a champion like Gino Bartali among its ranks filled me with such pride that my fear took a back seat."

As the war dragged on, the underground network struggled to find places to hide people. Then a doctor at a hospital in Rome came up with a brilliant idea. He invented a disease called "Il Morbo di K." He told the Nazi soldiers it was highly contagious so they would be too afraid to search the hospital. Some of the families waiting for Gino to bring them new exit papers may have been hiding in that hospital in Rome, thanks to Dr. Giovanni Borromeo and his imaginary disease.

When DELASEM leader Giorgio Nissim died, his sons found diaries filled with information about Gino Bartali's rescue efforts. Without these diaries, the world may never have known about Gino's work. And there is a reason for that. Gino did not want anyone to know.

"Those who have suffered in their soul, in their heart, in their spirit, in their mind, for their loved ones are the real heroes," Gino said. "I am just a cyclist."

# SOURCES


"Bartali honoured for saving Jews during the Holocaust," cyclingnews.com, January 28, 2012, www.cyclingnews.com/news/bartali-honoured-for-saving-jews-during-the-holocaust.

Bartali, Lisa (granddaughter of Gino Bartali), discussion with author, March 2018.

Bartali, Lisa. "My Grandfather Gino: Messenger of Peace: The Beginning of Underground Mission," February 13, 2018, www.biciclettami.it/en/my-grandfather-gino-messenger-of-peace-the-beginning-of-underground-trails.

"The Birth of the Champion," Museo del Ciclismo Gino Bartali, www.ciclomuseobartali.it/archivio/articolo1.html?id=9.

Bresci, Andrea (friend of Gino Bartali), discussion with author, April 14, 2018.

Bresci, Maurizio (son of Andrea Bresci, who was a friend of Gino Bartali), discussion with author, April 14, 2018.

Buck, Monica. "Gino Bartali: the Cycling Champion Who Helped the Jews Escape from the Nazis," welovecycling.com, September 7, 2017, www.welovecycling.com/wide/2017/09/07/gino-bartali-cycling-champion-helped-jews-escape-nazis.

"Campione Sui Pedali e Nella Vita. Gino Bartali Ricordato Ad Arezzo," TSD Tv Arezzo, January 27, 2016, www.youtube.com/watch?v=wU66uXzm5Zc.

Crutchley, Peter. "Gino Bartali: The cyclist who saved Jews in wartime Italy," bbc.com, May 9, 2014, www.bbc.com/news/magazine-27333310.

Davies, Lizzie. "Italy remembers cycling champion who helped save Jews from the Nazis," theguardian.com, July 17, 2014, www.theguardian.com/world/2014/jul/17/italy-remembers-gino-bartali-cycling-hero-save-jews-nazis.

Dirkdeklein. "Two Forgotten Heroes," History of Sorts, August 25, 2016, www. dirkdeklein.net/2016/08/25/two-forgotten-heroes.

"Don't Talk About It: Giorgio Goldenberg," Italy and the Holocaust Foundation, no date, www.italyandtheholocaust.org/dont-talk-about-it-Giorgio-Goldenberg-5.aspx.

"The Game of Their Lives: The Stories of Righteous Among the Nations Who Devoted Their Lives to Sport," www.yadvashem.org, no date, www.yadvashem.org/yv/en/exhibitions/righteous-sportsmen/bartali.asp.

Giddings, Caitlin. "Retracing the Route of Gino Bartali, Tour de France Champ and Holocaust Hero," bicycling.com, March 21, 2016, www.bicycling.com/rides/news/retracing-the-route-of-gino-bartali-tour-de-france-champ-and-Holocaust-hero.

"Gino Bartali: Righteous Among Nations," thepaceline.net, January 28, 2012, www.forums.thepaceline.net/printthread.php?t=103257&pp=40.

Goldenberg, Giorgio, interview by Oren Jacoby, *My Italian Secret: The forgotten Heroes*, Storyville Films, Hamptons International Film Festival, October 12, 2014.

Griggs, Mary Beth. "This Italian Cyclist Defied Fascists and Saved Lives," smithsonian.com, May 9, 2014, www.smithsonianmag.com/smart-news/italian-cyclist-defied-fascists-and-saved-lives-180951392.

Herlihy, David V. "Catching Up with Gino Bartali," bikeraceinfo.com, 1989, www.bikeraceinfo.com/riderhistories/gino-bartali.html.

Hurowitz, Richard. "A Cycling Legend's Secret War Mission: Saving Italy's Jews," thedailybeast.com, November 19, 2017, www.thedailybeast.com/a-cycling-legends-secret-war-mission-saving-italys-jews.

"Informe Robinson—El Secreto de Gino Bartali," Movistar+, June 15, 2015, www.youtube.com/watch?v=1UIJ1gV3cgE.

Leveille, David. "The incredible story of Italian cyclist Gino Bartali, who risked his life to rescue Jews during the Holocaust," pri.org, May 26, 2017, www.pri.org/stories/2017-05-26/incredible-story-italian-cyclist-gino-bartali-who-risked-his-life-rescue-jews.

MacMichael, Simon. "Gino Bartali hid Jewish family in Florence home to protect them from Holocaust," road.cc, December 28, 2010, www. road.cc/content/news/28770-gino-bartali-hid-jewish-family-florence-home-protect-them-holocaust.

Macur, Juliet. "Long-Ago Rivalry Still Stirs Passion at the Giro d'Italia," newyorktimes.com, May 18, 2009, www.nytimes.com/2009/05/19/sports/cycling/19cycling.html.

Masters, James. "Gino Bartali: The man who helped save Italy's Jews," cnn.com, October 29, 2014, www.edition.cnn.com/2014/10/29/sport/gino-bartali-saved-italys-jews/index.html.

McConnon, Aili. *Road to Valor: A True Story of WWII Italy, the Nazis, and the Cyclist Who Inspired a Nation*, Broadway Books, 2013.

McConnon, Aili and Andres McConnon. "Gino Bartali, Italian Cycling Legend, Saved Jews During WWII; Subject Of New Book: Road to Valor," huffingtonpost.com, June 19, 2012, www.huffingtonpost.com/2012/06/18/gino-bartali-italian-cycl_n_1597004.html.

"Rider Biographies: Gino Bartali," Cycling Hall of Fame, no date, www.cyclinghalloffame.com/riders/rider_bio.asp?rider_id=21.

Senzo, Angelo. "Gino Bartali: 'Righteous Among the Nations' Title," italiancyclingjournal.blogspot.com, November 7, 2010, www.italiancyclingjournal.blogspot.com/2010/11/gino-bartali-righteous-among-nations.html.

ibid., "Cycling Monuments, Memorials, Plaques, etc., Part III," italiancyclingjournal.blogspot.com, December 1, 2009, www.italiancyclingjournal.blogspot.com/2009/12/cycling-monuments-memorials-plaques-etc.html.

ibid., "More Gino Bartali Secrets Revealed," italiancyclingjournal.blogspot.com, December 30, 2010, www.italiancyclingjournal.blogspot.com/2010/12/more-gino-bartali-secrets-revealed.html.

Quill Tree Books is an imprint of HarperCollins Publishers.

Bartali's Bicycle: The True Story of Gino Bartali, Italy's Secret Hero
 For information address HarperCollins Children's Books, a division of HarperCollins Publishers, 195 Broadway, New York, NY 10007.
www.harpercollinschildrens.com

ISBN 978-0-06-290811-7

The artist used pencil and digital color to create the illustrations for this book.
Typography by Erin Fitzsimmons
22 23 24 RTLO 10 9 8 7 6 5 4 3 2

First Edition

"SOME MEDALS
ARE PINNED TO YOUR SOUL,
NOT YOUR JACKET."

GINO BARTALI
LE PEUPLE JUIF
RECONNAISSANT
QUICONQUE SAUVE UNE VIE SAUVE L'UNIVERS TOUT ENTIER

Bartali
Bartali